DOORS TO A WIDER PLACE
Stories from Australia

Australia is an enormous country, a wide place indeed, where many people have come to start new lives. One story looks at the early pioneer days in north-western Queensland; another shows life through the eyes of Punjabi children growing up by the Gwydir River in New South Wales. There are journeys of many different kinds: a father going back to look at his own childhood home, and a young Aboriginal man returning to his tribe after long years away. A woman makes another kind of journey, one that has no map, a journey to places in the mind where the line between the real and the unreal is no longer clear. And last, two brave teachers set out on an excursion to Sydney with twenty schoolgirls, who are determined to have fun day and night . . .

BOOKWORMS WORLD STORIES

English has become an international language, and is used on every continent, in many varieties, for all kinds of purposes. *Bookworms World Stories* are the latest addition to the Oxford Bookworms Library. Their aim is to bring the best of the world's stories to the English language learner, and to celebrate the use of English for storytelling all around the world.

Jennifer Bassett
Series Editor

Christine Lindop would like to thank the following for their assistance with the research for this volume: Virginia Gallagher in New Zealand; Vicky Eccott and staff at the British Empire and Commonwealth Museum, Bristol, UK

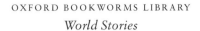

OXFORD BOOKWORMS LIBRARY
World Stories

Doors to a Wider Place

Stories from Australia

Stage 4 (1400 headwords)

Series Editor: Jennifer Bassett
Founder Editor: Tricia Hedge
Activities Editors: Jennifer Bassett and Christine Lindop

Who decides what is margin and what is text? Who decides where the borders of the homeland run? Absences and silences are potent. It is the eloquent margins which frame the official history of the land. As for geography, there are divisions and boundary lines that fissure any state more deeply than the moat it digs around the nationhood. In every country there are gaping holes. People fall through them and disappear. Yet on every side there are also doors to a wider place, a covert geography under sleep where all the waters meet.

Janette Turner Hospital
Australian novelist

RETOLD BY CHRISTINE LINDOP

Doors to a Wider Place

Stories from Australia

Illustrated by
Iain McKellar

OXFORD UNIVERSITY PRESS

OXFORD

UNIVERSITY PRESS

Great Clarendon Street, Oxford OX2 6DP

Oxford University Press is a department of the University of Oxford.
It furthers the University's objective of excellence in research, scholarship,
and education by publishing worldwide in

Oxford New York

Auckland Cape Town Dar es Salaam Hong Kong Karachi
Kuala Lumpur Madrid Melbourne Mexico City Nairobi
New Delhi Shanghai Taipei Toronto

With offices in

Argentina Austria Brazil Chile Czech Republic France Greece
Guatemala Hungary Italy Japan Poland Portugal Singapore
South Korea Switzerland Thailand Turkey Ukraine Vietnam

OXFORD and OXFORD ENGLISH are registered trade marks of
Oxford University Press in the UK and in certain other countries

ISBN: 978 0 19 479195 3

A complete recording of this Bookworms edition of *Doors to a Wider Place:
Stories from Australia* is available on audio CD ISBN 978 0 19 479162 5

Printed in Hong Kong

ACKNOWLEDGEMENTS

The publishers are grateful to the following for permission to adapt and simplify copyright texts:
the authors and Tom Thompson of Ett Imprint for 'Because of the Rusilla' from *The Time of the
Peacock* (1965) by Mena Abdullah & Ray Mathew; Meredith McKinney for 'The Weeping Fig' from
The Nature of Love (1966) by Judith Wright; the author and Allen and Unwin Pty. Ltd., Australia
for 'Going Home' by Archie Weller; Juanita Cragen (Curtis Brown Australia Pty. Ltd.) for 'The
Pepper-Tree' (1948) by Dal Stivens; to the author and Rogers Coleridge & White Ltd. (20 Powis
Mews, London W11 1JN) for 'The Empty Lunch-Tin' from *Antipodes* by David Malouf, reproduced
by permission of the author; the author for 'Cross Currents' from *The Hanged Man in the Garden*
(1989) by Marion Halligan

Word count (main text): 15,862 words

For more information on the Oxford Bookworms Library,
visit www.oup.com/elt/bookworms

CONTENTS

NOTE ON THE LANGUAGE

There are many varieties of English spoken in the world, and the characters in these stories sometimes use non-standard forms (for example, leaving out auxiliary verbs such as *am, are, is*). This is how the authors of the original stories represented the spoken language that their characters would actually use in real life.

There are also words that are usually only found in Australian English (for example, *humpy* and *stubbies*), and in the story by Archie Weller, an Aboriginal writer, there are a few words from one of the Aboriginal languages. All these words are either explained in the stories or in the glossary on page 72.

NOTE ON THE ILLUSTRATOR

Iain McKellar was born in Glasgow, Scotland, but has lived in Australia since he was six years old. Iain is an award-winning fine artist and illustrator, working in design, advertising, and educational publishing. These are his first illustrations for a book for English language learners.

Because of the Rusilla

MENA ABDULLAH AND RAY MATHEW

Retold by Christine Lindop

*Growing up in a new country means learning
a new way of life, and learning that, outside
the safety of your loving family, not everybody
is friendly.*

*Rashida, Nimmi (who tells the story), and
Lal are Punjabi children growing up on a farm
in Australia. Their first trip to town brings new
experiences for them all – some good, some
bad, some very surprising . . .*

The whole day – the trip to town, the nigger word, the singing kettle – was because of the Rusilla. It had flown away.

It was a small bird, and of no use to the farm, but it was Lal's, and losing it was a sad and terrible thing.

It was Rashida who found it, though, Rashida and I. It was in the grass by the river, shining red and green and trying to fly out of the long grass. I saw it first and I pointed to it. But Rashida followed it quietly and caught it. Then we carried it back to Father. Well, Rashida carried it. I wanted to, and anyway I saw it first, but Rashida did not offer and I could not ask her. She was older than I was and it was for her to decide. And although we were only children on the banks of the Gwydir, we were still Punjabis and Punjabis do not beg.

Father looked at the bird. 'Young and weak,' he said. 'Young and weak. It will mostly die.'

'Yes,' said Rashida, in a proud voice, trying to look at life in the Punjabi way. 'It will die.'

She gave the bird to me then and I took it gladly. I held it tightly, too tightly probably. Its wings moved wildly in my hands, and I could feel underneath them a wild beating, and I knew it was the bird's heart.

So I held it more gently than before in a cage of fingers. 'What bird?' I said. 'What sort of bird? What name?'

Father looked at me. I was always asking names, more names than there were words for. I was the dreamy child, the one he called the Australian.

'Rusilla,' he said at last. 'It is a bird called Rusilla.'

'Rusilla?' I said. 'Rusilla.' It was a good name and I was happy with it.

I took it home and showed it to Lal, who was only four.

'I have a Rusilla,' I said. 'It is a very strange bird, young and weak, and it will mostly die, but you can help me to find food for it.'

He went off, his face serious, while I put the bird in a cage where chickens had once lived in the garden. And from that day it was our job, Lal's and mine, to look for food in the garden for the Rusilla.

The garden was a strange place and lovely. It was our mother's place, Ama's own place. Outside the walls was the farm, with the sheep, the chickens, and Sulieman the rooster, the place where Father worked, and beyond that the Australian hills, with their changing faces. We had never been to them, and Ama — that was our word for 'mother'; *ama* means love — Ama told us they were very strange. But everything was strange to Ama, except the garden.

Inside the walls grew the country that she knew. It was cool and sweet and rich with the smell of flowers, jasmine like little stars, white violets, and the pink Kashmiri roses as tightly closed as a baby's fists. The kitchen smell of Punjabi cooking had no meaning in that place. There was Shah-Jehan the white peacock too. And other birds came there, free birds, the magpie that woke us at morning and sang us to bed at night, and a shining black bird that Indians call 'kokila' and Australians call 'koel'. But these were singing birds, that came and went, came and went. For the Rusilla, the garden was a cage.

It was a cage for Lal, too. He was gentle and small and the only son, because another older son had died soon after he opened his eyes. Ama and Father were afraid for Lal; they kept him in the garden. Rashida and I could run wild by the river, bare feet and screaming voices, but Lal could not go out without an adult. He had to live in the garden with the baby, Jamila, who was only six months old and who spent all day with her fist in her mouth, watching the rose leaves against the sky, or sleeping and sleeping. How could he play with her? To Lal the Rusilla was a bird, a friend, from heaven.

And it was completely his. As soon as it was well I lost interest in it. I told him that he could have it, that it was no use anyway, and it would never do anything except walk around in its cage. Lal did not care. He loved it and watched it for hours.

To Lal the Rusilla was a bird, a friend, from heaven.
He loved it and watched it for hours.

And then one morning, just like any other morning, we woke up and it was gone. The door of the cage was open and Salome the cat had disappeared. The magpies went on singing, and Lal shook his fist at them as he'd seen Father shake his fist at the sun. And he cried.

How he cried! Tears down his face, and no sound. And all the time he ran round the garden – now quick, now slow – looking, looking. He did not even speak.

'Ama,' said Rashida, 'let Lal come to the river with us.'

'We'll show him the ducks,' I said. 'Baby ones, Lal.'

But it was no good. Ama told Father it was no good, and Father, smiling a little, held Lal in his arms for a long time. But the tears were still there, and all afternoon Father went round the farm trying to find a Rusilla. But the bird from heaven had gone.

We children slept in the same room and that night Rashida and I lay for a long time listening to Lal. At last we climbed out of the big bed and went over to him.

'Lal-baba,' said Rashida. 'Don't cry. Don't cry,' she said again, and I saw that there were tears on her cheek and I felt my eyes filling.

'Don't cry, don't cry, don't cry,' I said. And then I was crying, very loudly, and Rashida, with tears on her face, was annoyed with me, and Ama was suddenly there. She picked Lal up and held him like a very little baby.

'What noise!' she said. 'Go to bed.' Then she sat on a chair with Lal and talked to him in her soft Indian voice – so soft, and yet we heard her. 'My son,' she said. 'My son, no tears. Allah makes birds to fly. No tears. It is cruel, it is cruel to stay in a cage when you have the wings and the heart to fly. No tears. You cannot hold a bird. You cannot hold things, anything, my son.'

Lal sat close to her, his face hot from crying. Ama's face was tired, but suddenly she smiled and looked beautiful.

'Tomorrow,' she said, 'Seyed can take you in the wagon and you can see the town.'

'Me too, Ama? Me too?' Rashida and I jumped up in bed. None of us had ever been to town. Lal stopped crying.

'Yes, all of you,' said Ama. And she took Lal into her own room while Rashida and I whispered excitedly about Uncle Seyed, the Rusilla, and the town.

Uncle Seyed came next day with the wagon. It was always used on town days, but it was very old. It belonged to the time when Father first came to Australia. With the money from his first jobs he bought the wagon. It still had his name painted on the side.

We'd been in it lots of times, but never to go to town, never to go to town. We jumped about in the back while Seyed worried about us falling out. In the end he tried talking to us, hoping to make us stay still.

'Good land that,' he said. He always spoke to us in English, his sort of English. 'Long time ago I want your father to buy it, but no. He want go back home, get marry. I tell him he too young get marry, but no.' Seyed shook his head and Rashida laughed. She knew that Father was forty when he married. Seyed shook his head again. 'Always your father wanting to get marry.'

'When will you get married, Uncle Seyed?' asked Rashida.

'Plenty time yet,' said Seyed, who was in his fifties. 'Plenty time yet.'

'I will marry you,' I said. And then I thought a bit. 'Soon,' I added, and Rashida laughed.

And so the talking, the good time, went, while the sun got big and the houses came closer to one another. When we drove into the town we had no words to say.

Seyed stopped the wagon in the grass at the side of the road and lifted us down.

'Better you wait here, out of the sun,' he said. 'No run on road. Back in few minutes.' He shook a warning finger at us and left us.

It was only a small town, and we looked at it, looked hard.

'What's that?' I said, pointing to a high, high building.

'Only a Jesus-house,' said Rashida.

'Look!' said Lal suddenly. 'Rusilla.'

We looked. It was a stone rooster, near a stone man on the side of the building. It seemed very wonderful to us and we stood staring at it while Lal talked happily about Rusilla, the bird from heaven, and how it lived on a house.

It was because of the Rusilla and the stone man that we did not notice them. Suddenly they were there, white children – a big boy, a girl, and a little boy. We stared at them. They stared at us.

'What y' wearin' y' pyjamas in the street f'r?' said the big boy.

'What y' wearin' y' pyjamas in the street f'r?' said the girl.

We stared at them and I repeated the question in my head again and again like a song. 'What are you wearing your pyjamas in the street for?' I did not know what it meant, but I knew it was about our clothes. We were all dressed alike in the salwar kameez, a kind of loose top and cotton trousers. They were cheap to buy and easy to make. Why were they pointing, and singing, and saying such sharp pointy words?

'Nigger,' sang the big boy. 'Nigger, nigger, pull the trigger.'

'Nigger, nigger, pull the trigger,' said the others. They were all saying it, singing it, like a game.

'Game!' cried Lal. He lived in a world of women, an only son, and here were boys. He ran to meet them.

The big boy caught him around the waist and threw him backwards to the ground. I looked at him there, sitting up surprised, and felt my legs shaking.

'*Sur ka bucha!*' said Rashida. '*Sur ka bucha!*' she screamed and threw herself at the boy, hitting at him with her fists. My mouth fell open, because that means 'son of a pig', and it was a terrible thing to say, but I followed her, crying '*Sur! Sur!*' And, jumping at the girl, I got two handfuls of hair.

We were all there fighting – kicking and hitting with Lal sitting surprised on the ground – when Seyed came back.

'Ai! Ai!' he cried as he turned the corner and began to run. At the sound of his voice the fighting stopped and the strangers ran away. Rashida stood looking after them, strong and angry, but I looked towards Seyed.

He asked us what had happened and I held up a fist that had some light-coloured hair in it and started to cry. And, of course, that made Lal cry too; he couldn't let any of us cry alone. Seyed tried hard to be calm. He picked Lal up and brushed the dust off him. He made my hair tidy and told Rashida, who was too proud to cry, to wipe her nose.

'Take us home,' commanded Rashida. 'Take us home now.'

'Business at bank. No go home yet.' But he could see that Rashida was close to tears too, so he hurried us into the wagon and drove us down the street. We lay down in the back and none of us looked out.

'Where are we going?' I said, but in a very little voice that Seyed could not hear. Rashida sat up and looked.

'We are not going home,' she said, and her voice trembled. But she stayed sitting up, looking proud. As I lay there crying into Lal's hair, I thought that she looked very like Father and wondered if anybody would ever think that about me.

Seyed took us to a little house on the other side of town where a white lady lived. He told us to stay with her and to give her no trouble because she was a friend, and that if we were good he would come back and take us home soon. Then he went away, into the town, while we stood in the garden and looked at the ground.

'I don't know your names,' said the lady.

Rashida was the eldest. 'I am Rashida Bani. This is my sister, Nimmi Kushil. And this is my brother – the only son – Lal Muhummad. We come from Simla Farm.'

'I know it,' said the lady. 'I knew it, and I knew your father before you were thought of.' We stared at her politely; she must be very old. We could not imagine a time when father and Ama had not thought of us, and wanted us.

She took us into the house and, like a kind and sensible woman, she went on with her work and left us alone. We walked round slowly, in sight of one another, and looked at everything. Then we decided.

Rashida stood by the piano. She touched a key. A wonderful thing happened. A note came loud and clear. Then it died away, but you knew that it would never go because you had it in your mind and in your heart. She touched another one and, after the note started, sang with it. There were two notes then, the same and different, but again the piano note died away into your mind. Lal laughed and I stood listening while Rashida tried different notes. High notes some of them were and some were low, and she sang with all of those she could. She was always singing at home and she knew all of Ama's songs.

I sat on the floor near her and turned over the pages of a magazine. The pages shone, and they smelt beautiful. There were big pictures, and I put my head close to them to see them and smell them and really know them.

Lal began talking to a black cat that was sleeping under the table. He talked happily for a long time, but the cat woke up and walked off into another room. Lal followed him.

Suddenly there was a whistling noise and a shout from Lal. Such a shout! Rashida and I jumped up and ran after him. He was in the kitchen, standing in front of the cooker. On it was a kettle, a kettle that sang. He pointed to it.

'Look,' he said. 'Listen.' We could not believe it. We all three stood there with our eyes wide in surprise. A kettle that sang, sang with a sharp, high sound.

'Like a bird,' said Rashida.

'Magic,' said I.

We all three stood there with our eyes wide in surprise.
A kettle that sang . . .

'Rusilla,' said Lal.

The lady came in and took the kettle off the cooker. 'It sings to say that the water is hot,' she said. 'I saw your uncle coming up the street and put it on to make some tea.'

So we all sat down to tea and cakes and talked like one big family. We loved the lady now, the kind lady with the piano and the magazines, the cat and the kettle. We told her about the farm, about the Rusilla and the garden where Lal lived, about Jamila the baby and the long time she was asleep. We told her everything and she listened and laughed and smiled while Seyed drank cups of black tea full of sugar. And Lal talked too. He talked to Seyed and told him, very seriously, about the wonderful kettle that sang like a bird.

Then we all went out to the wagon. We stood for a moment in the garden to say goodbye and the lady picked two roses and gave a strong red one to Rashida and a dear pink one to me.

'For good girls,' she said. Then she looked at Lal and shook her head. 'I can't give flowers to a man.'

Lal's face fell and we were afraid that he would cry, but he just looked sad and Seyed lifted him into the wagon.

'Don't go,' said the lady. 'Wait.' And she went inside.

We were all in the wagon ready to go when she came out. She was carrying the kettle.

'This is for you,' she said and held it towards Lal. 'I have two others for myself.'

Lal took it, but Seyed gave him a look full of meaning, and he half held it out for her to take back. Even Lal knew that Punjabi men do not accept presents easily.

'Let him take it,' said the lady. 'A friend gives you what is already your own.'

Seyed thought about it and then smiled, a great big smile. 'You Punjabi lady,' he said.

So the kettle was Lal's. All the way home we held our presents, even when we went to sleep. But we woke up near home. We climbed up near Seyed, who worried that we would fall off. We heard him asking Allah to keep us safe until he got us home to Father.

The sun was going down as we saw our home. The day was coming to an end. The birds flew off towards the trees, and there were little sleepy night noises from the animals. There was a smell of wood smoke and cooking, and there, there by the door, with the baby on her arm and a light in her hand, was Ama.

'No more,' said Seyed Muhammad seriously (but not truthfully) as he helped us down from the wagon. 'No more will I take these terrible children into town, as long as Allah lets me live.'

We laughed at him, and we held our roses up for Ama to smell. But Lal pushed between us.

'Look, Ama,' he said, holding up his kettle. 'Rusilla.'

The Weeping Fig

JUDITH WRIGHT

Retold by Christine Lindop

Sometimes the present is not enough; people need to connect to the past – to know the history of their family, who they were, where they came from, how they lived . . .

In north-western Queensland a man comes looking for his past. Here, the sun bakes the land dry and hard, and the hot air burns the eyes. How can people – or trees – survive in this terrible heat?

'Only tinned milk, I'm afraid, Mr Condon. When you live in a place like this you have to expect that,' the woman was saying. She held the teapot high in the air, waiting for his answer.

'Oh – no, no milk, thank you.' Looking out at that unwelcoming landscape he had forgotten about her for a moment. Now he turned towards her and made an attempt at conversation. Though it was really too hot to join in her tea party silliness. The woman had even changed her dress!

'Have you always lived here, Mrs Hastings?'

'Oh no. Harold came here as manager two years ago – that was before I married him. I had no idea he lived in a place like this! We hope for a city job as soon as we can find a house. Of course, the pay *is* good, it's true. But seventy

miles from the nearest town – and such a town! And to tell
the truth, Mr Condon, I don't think country life is right for
someone like me. My old home, you see, was down by the
river, quite close to the city shops – right in the middle of
things. But Charlotte Downs – I always say, "The best view
of Charlotte Downs is in your mirror when you drive away."'

He laughed politely. 'Who really owns this place, then?'

'Oh, it's run by a company, like most of these old places.
No one would choose to live here, would they? I don't know
how long they've had it. We get a visit now and then from
someone important – big cars, you know, and good clothes
– but only in the cool season.' She gave an angry little laugh.
'They don't have to know what the rest of the year is like,
now do they?'

'You don't know, then, whether any of the original
buildings are still standing?'

She looked bored. 'No, I've never asked. But Bertha might
know – she's always worked in the house here. Her father
worked here with the cattle all his life. If you want to ask
her . . .'

'Well, yes, I have a special reason, you see,' he began to
explain. But she was not interested in his reasons.

'Bertha,' she called towards the dark rooms beyond the
verandah. 'Come here a minute.'

There was a pause, then a door behind him opened, and
he turned. Bertha came forward – any age over thirty, deep
brown skin, barefoot, in an ugly dress, moving with painful
slowness on a thin, stick-like leg.

'Yes, Missus?'

'Mrs Hastings, please, Bertha. I've told you before. This gentleman here, Mr Condon, would like to know something about the buildings here.' She took out a cigarette and turned impatiently away.

Bertha waited.

'I was just asking Mrs Hastings' – Condon said uncomfortably – 'whether any of the original buildings are left, the ones that were first built here.'

Bertha lifted a thin arm. 'Out there, by the big green tree, you see?'

'Yes,' Condon answered.

'That the old homestead, my father told me years ago. See, made of slab. They use that one for store – wood, paint, that kind of thing. Nearly fallen down, you see.'

'Did your father – did he ever tell you anything about the people who built that hut? People called Condon?'

Bertha's face showed nothing. 'No, didn't say. I got things cooking, Missus – Hastings. Think I better go and look.'

Mrs Hastings turned to Condon, her bright earrings dancing wildly. 'Do you have any more questions, Mr Condon?'

Condon shook his head and thanked Bertha. There was nothing left here now. The years, the dust of the dry seasons, the wet of the rainy seasons had washed away everything that had been. But still – he would like to look at the building before he went.

'Tell me,' Mrs Hastings asked, only a little interested, 'how long ago were your people here?'

'My great-grandfather left here in eighteen sixty-five.'

'My goodness,' Mrs Hastings said. 'And you're still interested in it. Would you like to go and look at the building, perhaps?'

Condon stood up. 'Yes, thank you. I'll have to leave soon though. I have an appointment in the town tonight.'

'Please consider the place your own,' Mrs Hastings said. 'I shan't come out; it's really too hot. But do come back to say goodbye. We don't get many visitors here.' Her eyes said clearly that this visitor had been a real disappointment.

Condon walked down the steps and turned towards the old building. As he left the shade of the verandah, the heat took his breath away. November was the worst month to travel in north-western Queensland, he thought. If his company sent him up here again on business, he would try to get out of it. It was the name of the town – Hambleton – that had made him stop. So it's still here, he had thought, Hambleton, the name that had come into the old diary, the writing now a pale red, like dried blood on the page. So the places were real. He would go and see.

The little building was leaning crazily now, but it had been honestly built, he could see. He remembered the story of the work, written in the diary, month after month: choosing the trees, cutting them down, making the slabs, joining them together, then putting the roof on and making the floor.

♀

Ellen and the children moved into the house yesterday. A great change from the wagon, and they are delighted. The future looks good, and the cattle are doing well.

♀

He bent down to look at the woodwork, nearly a century old – yes, old Stephen Condon had known his job. 'But what would I know about that?' he said to himself sadly. For it seemed to him suddenly that Stephen had been proud of his work in a way that he himself had never known.

Inside, the building was full of all kinds of unwanted rubbish, left there by different owners and managers over the years. Two old wagon-wheels leaned in a corner; there were slabs of wood, mysterious bits of old metal, wooden posts, ropes, empty boxes, dirt, broken things, forgotten things – all covered with thick white dust. The inside of the house had disappeared under the rubbish.

He could see the place where the window had been. This was where he saw Ellen, his great-grandmother, who had come alive to him through the pages of the diary. Here she had sat and sewed; here she had leaned, weak with sickness, while her two children burned with fever in their rough beds; here she had known loneliness, fear, happiness. Ellen – seventeen when she married, twenty when she came to Australia from the soft green hills of Devonshire, twenty-two when she died, Ellen who had loved birds and saved bits of bread for them, who hated snakes and lost her daughter through snakebite. And there by the chimney was a rough table. He imagined Stephen cutting the wood, making the table, giving it to Ellen.

But the heat in the little hut drove him back to the door. He leaned on the outside of the door trying to breathe, and looked out beyond the homestead buildings to the thin sickly trees and the burning hot earth.

Pioneers. What rubbish people talked about them. In the end pioneers were human beings like anyone else – they weren't finer people, or stronger, or better. Nobody would choose to live in a place like this if they could avoid it, he could imagine Mrs Hastings saying. Or had people really been different then? Did they find deeper meaning, greater purpose, in their lives – more than Mrs Hastings and he, John Condon, had ever known? It was useless to ask – you couldn't know any more than the old diary told you.

And what did it say about this crazy hut, falling down next to him? Death, death, and again death; hope lost, and brought back to life; loneliness, ugliness, the hunger that promises death – and then that last handwritten cry: *My wife is dead.* Not her name; no more was said; the diary ended.

It was by chance that he had found out the rest, down in the hot northern town by the sea, when he spent some time looking at old newspapers. Stephen Condon's dream had come to a cruel end; he had gone from Charlotte Downs, leaving nothing but graves behind. He had ridden, carrying his one remaining son, three hundred miles to that northern town, and died there.

What happened after that? John Condon had no idea. Only the diary remained, found among old papers when his own father died. On its cover his father had written 'Diary of my grandfather?' And so Stephen Condon had disappeared behind question marks into a lost past.

And why had he, John Condon, come here anyway? Nothing had come out of this but a headache. Did he want to come back here, to this terrible heat, where your eyes

burned in your head? If he could afford to buy this place
– and certainly he could not – no, he really did not want to.
He leaned against the door, looking for shade. He would
go as soon as he could find that woman and say goodbye.
Death! The place was full of it.

But round the wall of the hut there was shade. In a world
of burning heat and light he saw a place of darkness, and he
went towards it thankfully. Then he looked up and saw the
thick green leaves waving gently above him, making a cave
of coolness. It was a weeping fig tree.

Today Ellen planted the Port Jackson fig. It seems impossible,
but she has kept it alive all the way in the wagon. We plan
for our old age a seat and a table under it, though it is now
just one foot high. It will make wonderful shade for our
garden . . .

A terrible, cruel day for us both. Today we buried little Jane
near the fig tree. Ellen says she must have her near to the
house . . .

Ellen had a son last night, but he died at birth. She is heart-
broken, and very weak. One son remains to us . . .

A crazy journey – a journey of the heart, not the head. Yet
he could not help feeling, as he looked up into the tree's
blue-green shadows, a kind of triumph. 'Well,' he said to
himself, though he did not really know why, 'that was worth
coming for.' Yes, that fig tree. It had survived. It was alive,

John Condon looked up and saw the thick green leaves waving gently above him, making a cave of coolness.

it was green; in that empty hard landscape it triumphed. And those dead Condons had given their red blood to make this green living thing. The tree was taller than anything he could see. The Condons and the landscape – here they met. It was a root – it was what he had wanted.

Mrs Hastings walked slowly across the dry grassless earth; her big wide sunhat was a bright, shiny pink.

'Do come and have a drink before you go, Mr Condon. You've been here nearly an hour! I thought the sun had made you ill.'

Suddenly he pointed towards the tree. 'My great-grandmother and two of her children are buried under that tree.' Now why had he said that? He was proud of the fact, he realized.

Mrs Hastings screamed a little. 'But how terrible! Now I've really had too much of this place. I go cold all over when I think about graves. Do come back to the house. My husband will be back in a little while; he would so much like to meet you, I'm sure.'

Driving away, John Condon was the businessman again. He had not much time to get to the town for that appointment. Tall and proud above the dying landscape, the weeping fig waved its leaves in triumph, but he did not look back. He had got what he had come for.

Going Home

ARCHIE WELLER

Retold by Christine Lindop

Home for some of the Aboriginal people of Australia means a camp out of town, away from places where white people live.

William Jacob Woodward (Billy) is going home to the camp where he grew up, home from the city where he has been a successful Aboriginal painter and football star in the whites' world. But five years is a long time to be away from home . . .

> *I want to go home*
> *I want to go home*
> *Oh, Lord, I want to go home.*

The singer's voice comes from a cassette and slides out past the top of the window, out into the world of magpies' songs, and a darkness full of night spirits.

The man does not know that world. His is the world of the shiny new car, the big Kingswood travelling fast down the road.

At last he can be proud, and walk with his head high as his ancestors did many years before him. He had his first show a month ago. His paintings sold well, and with the money from them he bought the car.

Black hands move the shiny black wheel round a corner. For five years he has worked hard and saved, and now, on his twenty-first birthday, he is going home. New car, new clothes, new life. He takes a cigarette from the packet beside him, and lights it. His hair is tidy, his clothes are clean.

Billy Woodward is coming home, strong and proud, like a soldier returning from war.

Sixteen years old. Last year at school.

His little brother Carlton and his cousin Rennie Davis, down beside the river, on that last night before he went to the college in Perth, when all three had had a goodbye drink, with their girls beside them. Silent hot air, and moonlight on the river. Voices whispering and giggling. The clink of beer bottles.

That year at college, with all its schoolwork, and learning, everybody doing the same things the same way – but when it came to football, Billy was different.

Black hands grab the ball. Black feet kick the ball. Black hopes rise up with the ball to the sickly white sky.

No one can stop him now. He forgets about the river, and the people of his blood, and the girl in his heart.

When he was eighteen, he was picked by a top city team. That was the year that he played for West Australia, when he was named best player. That was a year to remember.

He never went out to the camp at Guildford, so he never saw his people: his dark, silent, staring people, his noisy, fighting, drunk people. *He* was white now.

William Jacob Woodward finished his fifth year with excellent results. All the teachers were proud of him. He went to the West Australian Institute of Technology to study painting. He bought bright clean clothes and cut off his long hair that all the camp girls had loved.

Billy was a handsome young man, with the nose and chin of his white grandfather and the quietness of his Aboriginal ancestors. He stood tall and proud, with the sensitive lips of a dreamer and calm golden-brown eyes.

He went to nightclubs regularly and sat alone in a dark corner, or with a painted white girl. He would drink wine, and watch the white tribe dancing to the wild music.

He was walking home one night when a middle-aged Aboriginal woman came out of a side street, and half-fell against him, her hands grabbing at his shirt. She laughed drunkenly up into his face.

'Billy! Ya Billy Woodward, unna?'

'Yes. What of it?' he said coldly.

'Ya dunno me? I'm ya Aunty Rose, from down Koodup.' She laughed again. Ugly, oh so ugly. Yellow and red eyes, broken teeth, dirty grey hair.

His people.

He pushed her away and walked off quickly. But he remembered her face for many days afterwards, whenever he tried to paint a picture. He felt ashamed that a thing like that was of his blood, his tribe.

That was his life: painting pictures and playing football and pretending. But his people knew. They always knew.

In his latest game of football he played against a young part-Aboriginal boy who stared at him through the whole game with large black eyes.

After the game, the boy's family arrived in a big old car. Billy, standing with his white friends, saw them from a distance. He saw the children kicking an old football about with shouts of laughter, and two tall boys by the car talking to the young footballer, a pretty girl leaning out the car window, and an old couple in the back. The three boys looked up and saw Billy – fashionable Billy, with his white friends. Their smiles died for a moment as their proud black eyes cut through him like knives.

So Billy was going home, because he had been reminded of home at that last match.

It's raining now. Night time – the time when woodarchis come out to kill, leaving no marks on the ground behind them, passing like cloud shadows over the sun.

Trees dance in the half-light. Strange black shapes with great untidy heads and long, reaching arms. Ancestors crying *Remember me*. Voices shriek or whisper tiredly: tired from the countless warnings that are not listened to. Billy cannot understand these trees. They pull him onwards, even when he thinks of turning back and not going home – a place he once promised himself he would never go back to again.

A shape steps into the road at the Koodup crossroads.

An Aboriginal man.

Billy stops the car, or he will run the man over.

Door opens.

Wind and rain and coloured man get in.

'Ta, mate. It's bloody cold 'ere,' he says, then looks at Billy with sharp black eyes. 'Nyoongah, are ya, mate?'

'Yes.'

'Well, I'm Darcy Goodrich.'

He holds out a rough hand, yellow-brown, dirty. A lifetime of sadness is held between the fingers.

Billy takes the hand. 'I'm William Woodward.'

'Yeah?' The eyes look all over him again. 'You goin' anywhere near Koodup, William?'

'Yes.'

'Good-oh. This is a nice car ya got. Ya must have plenty of boya, unna?'

Silence from Billy.

He would rather not have this cold wet man beside him, reminding him. He keeps his golden-brown eyes on the road.

'Got a smoke, William?'

'Certainly. Help yourself.'

Black fingers open his expensive cigarette case.

'Ya want one too, mate?'

'Thanks.'

'Ya wouldn't be Teddy Woodward's boy, would ya, William?'

'Yes, that's right. How are Mum and Dad, and everyone?'

Suddenly he has to know all about his family and become lost in a sea of brownness.

Darcy looks at him in surprise, then turns back to the window. He smokes his cigarette quietly.

'What, ya don't know?' he says softly. 'Ya Dad was drinkin'. Blind drunk, he was. Well, this car came out of nowhere when 'e was crossin' the road on a night like this. Never seen 'im. Never stopped or nothing. Ya brother Carl found 'im next day an' there was nothing no one could do then. That was a couple of years back now.'

A couple of years back – so when Billy was nineteen, a football star. On one of those bright white nights, when he was living the good life with wine and white women, Billy's father had been taken off the face of his country – all alone.

He can remember his father as a small gentle man who could cheat at cards better than anybody in the camp. He could make boats out of duck feathers, and he and Carlton and Billy had had races by the waterhole, from where his people had come long ago, in the time of the beginning.

The lights of Koodup shine out at him as he comes round a bend.

'Tell ya what, mate. Stop at the hotel and buy a box of stubbies.'

'All right, Darcy.' Billy smiles and looks closely at the man for the first time. He desperately feels that he needs a friend as he goes back into the open mouth of his old life.

'Ya must want to see ya people again, unna?' says Darcy.

His people: ugly Aunty Rose, his dead forgotten father, his wild brother and cousin. Even this silent man. They are all his people.

He can never escape.

The car stops beside the hotel, and the two Nyoongah run through the rain into the hard light of the small hotel bar.

The barman is a long time coming, although the bar is almost empty. Grey eyes stare at Billy.

*The barman is a long time coming, although the bar
is almost empty.*

'A box of stubbies, please.'

'Only if you bastards drink it down at the camp. Police told me you lot are drinking in town and just causing trouble.'

'We'll drink where we bloody like, thanks, mate.'

'Will you, you little bastard?' The barman looks at Billy in surprise. 'Well then, you're not getting nothing from me. You can get out of here before I call the police. They'll tell you what you can and can't do, you clever black bastard.'

Something hits Billy deep inside so strongly that he wants to grab the bar and be sick.

He is black, and the barman is white, and nothing can ever change that.

All the time he had enjoyed the wine and the nightclubs and the fashionable clothes and the smiles of white women; he had played the white man's game better than most of the wadgulas, and painted his country in white man colours with the wadgulas all talking nonsense about it; all this time he had thought he was someone better than his tribe.

But in the end, he is just a black man.

Darcy moves quietly to the angry barman's side.

''Scuse me, Mr Owett, but William 'ere just come 'ome, see,' he says. He is a dog with its tail between its legs. 'We *will* be drinking in the camp, you know.'

'Just come home, eh? What was he in prison for?'

Billy bites his reply back so it stays, hard and hurtful, in his stomach.

'Well, all right, Darcy. I'll forget about it this time. Just don't let your friend annoy me again.'

Out into the rain again. They drive away and turn down

a rough road about a kilometre out of town. Darcy opens a bottle and gives it to Billy.

'Act stupid, mate, and ya go a lo-ong way in this town.'

Billy takes a long drink of the bitter golden beer. It is like sunshine after a storm. He begins to calm down.

'Hey, Darcy, I'm twenty-one today.'

Darcy gives Billy a big smile and puts his hand out.

'Twenty-bloody-one, eh? 'Ow's it feel?'

'No different from yesterday.'

Billy shakes Darcy's hand.

They laugh and drink to his birthday as they drive into the camp. Dark and wet, with a wild wind, and rain beating down on the shapeless humpies. Darcy points to a humpy at the edge of the camp.

'That's where ya mum lives.'

A rough shape made of pieces of metal and wood. Two bags, sewn together, make a door. Everywhere there are tins, bits of toys or cars, and mud.

Billy stops as close to the door as he can. He had forgotten what his house really looked like.

'Come on, mate. Come an' see ya ole mum. Ya might be lucky too, an' catch ya brother.'

Billy can't say anything. He gets slowly out of the car, and this lonely, broken place reaches out to take hold of him.

He is one of the brotherhood.

He follows Darcy through the bag door. He feels unsure and terribly alone.

There are six people: two old women, a very old man, two young men, and a shy young woman, who is expecting a baby. The young man nearest the door looks up with an empty yellowish face. His long black hair is held off his face by a piece of red cotton – red for the earth of his ancestors' lands, red for the blood that fell on the land when the white tribe came. Red, the only bright thing in this dark, dull place.

The young man gives a weak smile at Darcy and the beer.

'G'day, Darcy. 'Oo ya mate is?'

''Oo'd ya think, Carl, ya stupid bastard? 'E's ya brother, come home.'

Carlton stares at Billy, not believing Darcy. Then his smile widens a little and he stands up, putting his hand out. They shake hands and stare deep into each other's faces, smiling. Happiness goes quietly from one to the other.

Then his cousin Rennie, tall and thin with reddish hair and grey eyes, shakes hands. He introduces Billy to his young woman, Phyllis, and reminds him that old China Groves and Florrie Waters are his mother's parents.

His mother sits silently at the kitchen table. One of her eyes is sightless; the other stares at her son, but there is no welcoming light in it. She is too proud to show her pain.

From this woman I came, Billy thinks, like a flower from the ground. From this camp I flew away.

He remembers his mother as a laughing brown woman, with long black hair, singing softly as she cleaned the house or cooked food. Now she is old and stupid in her sadness.

'So ya came back after all. Ya couldn't come back when we buried ya Dad, unna? Ya think ya too good for ya old family, I s'pose,' she whispers in a thin voice before Billy even says hello. Then she turns her eyes back into her pain.

'It's my birthday, Mum. I wanted to see everybody. No one told me Dad was dead.'

Carlton looks up at Billy.

'I think ya must be twenty-one, Billy.'

'Yes.'

'Well, we just gotta have a party,' Carlton smiles. 'We gotta get more drink.'

Carlton and Rennie drive off to town in Billy's car. When they leave, Billy feels unsure and alone. His mother just stares at him. Phyllis says nothing, and the grandparents talk to Darcy, camp talk that Billy cannot understand.

The cousins come back through the door with a box that Carlton drops on the table, then he turns to his brother. His face has a look like a small child waiting to show his father what he has made. His dark lips are trying not to smile.

''Appy birthday, Billy, ya ole bastard,' Carlton says, and brings a shining gold watch out of the pocket of his jeans.

'It even works, Billy,' says Rennie from beside his woman, and Darcy and China laugh.

The laughter dances around the room like dead leaves from a tree.

They drink. They talk. Darcy goes home and the old people go to bed. His mother has not talked to Billy all night. In the morning he will buy her some pretty curtains for the windows, and make a proper door, and buy her the best dress in the shop.

They remember good times. Soon Billy is not William Woodward the football star and artist, but Billy the wild boy, with his big smile and a crowd of girls round his sweet body.

''Appy birthday, Billy,' Carlton says, and brings a shining
gold watch out of the pocket of his jeans.

Here they are – all three together again, but now young Rennie is almost a father, and Carlton has just come back from three months in prison. And Billy? He is nowhere.

At last Carlton stands up.

'Time for bed.' He hits his brother gently on the shoulder. 'See ya tomorrow, Billy.' He smiles.

Billy lies down in a blanket and stares at the dying fire. In his mind he can hear the voice of his father, telling stories, and the voice of his mother, singing. Soon he is asleep.

He wakes to the sound of magpies in the still trees. He gets up off the floor and goes quietly to the door.

Carlton's eyes look out from the blankets on his bed.

'Where ya goin'?' he whispers.

'Just for a walk.'

'See ya later, Billy,' he smiles sleepily. Billy goes outside.

A watery sun comes up over the hills and shines down on the camp. Broken glass, catching the sunlight, looks white, like the bones of dead animals. Several young men stand around looking at Billy's car. He waves at them and they wave back. After a wash Billy goes to the waterhole. He wants – a lot – to remember his father.

He stands there, watching the light rain falling on the green water. Bird song from the green-brown-black trees nearby is sharp and clear. Then he wanders back to the humpy. Smoke from fires is climbing up into the grey sky.

Just as he arrives at the edge of the camp, a police car pushes its way in through the mud and rubbish. A hard white face looks out at him. The car stops.

'Hey, you! Come here!'

The people at the fires watch, from the corners of their eyes, as he goes slowly over.

'That your car?'

'Yes.' Billy stares at the heavy police sergeant in his blue uniform. Next to him is the driver, another policeman.

'What's your name, and where'd you get the car?' the driver says.

'I just told you, it's my car. My name's William Jacob Woodward, if it's any business of yours,' Billy says angrily.

The sergeant gets slowly out of the car. He looks down at black Billy, who suddenly feels small and weak.

'You Carlton's brother?'

'If you want to know—'

'I want to know, you black bastard. I want to know everything about you,' the sergeant says.

'Yeah, like where you were last night when the store was robbed, as soon as you come home causing trouble in the pub,' the driver says.

'I wasn't causing trouble, and I wasn't in any robbery. I like the way you come straight down here when there's trouble—'

'If you weren't in the robbery, what's this watch?' The sergeant is delighted, and he grabs Billy's hand that has painted so many beautiful pictures for the wadgula people. He pushes it up behind Billy's back and throws him against the car. The golden watch hangs between the pink fingers.

'Listen, I was here. You can ask my grandparents or Darcy Goodrich.' But inside Billy knows it is no good.

'Don't give me that. When there's trouble, you bastards stay together like flies round a toilet,' the driver says.

Nothing matters any more. Not the trees, throwing their thin arms wide and free. Not the people round their warm fires. Not the rain going down the back of his neck onto his skin. Just this heavy man and the shiny machine with POLICE written neatly on the side.

'You black bastard, I'm going to make you – and your bloody brother – jump. You nearly killed old Peters last night,' the big man says. Then the driver is beside him, staring angrily from behind his sunglasses.

'You Woodwards are all the same, thieving bastards. If you think you're such a fighter, beating up old men, you can try the sergeant here when we get back to the station.'

'Let's get the other one now, Morgan,' says the sergeant. 'Mrs Riley said there were two of them.'

Billy is pushed roughly into the back of the car, and sits there miserably as the car drives over to the humpy. Sees his new Kingswood standing in the mud. Darcy, a frightened Rennie, and several others stand by it, watching with lifeless eyes. Billy sees the policemen pull his brother from the humpy, his eyes sad, staring down at the ground.

He is thrown into the back of the car.

Carlton gives Billy a tired look, then gives his strange, weak smile.

'Welcome 'ome, brother,' he says quietly.

The Pepper-Tree

DAL STIVENS

Retold by Christine Lindop

When we look back to childhood, we usually think about the happy times – the home where we grew up, the games we played, the dreams we had.

Young Joe is growing up in the city, but his father has fond memories of his own childhood in a small country town. Joe listens to his father's stories, and imagines the great pepper-tree in the backyard...

My father often spoke about the pepper-tree when I was a child, and it was clear that it meant a lot to him – like the Rolls Royce he was always going to buy. It wasn't what he said about the pepper-tree – my father was not very clever with words – but how he said it. When he spoke of the pepper-tree at Tullama where he had grown up, you saw it clearly: an enormous tree with long sheets of green leaves in a big wide backyard in a country town.

'A proper backyard – not one of your miserable city yards,' my father said. In this great tree there was always a noisy traffic of birds flying from branch to branch.

When we lived at Newtown, Sydney, I used to look for pepper-trees when my father took me for a walk on Sunday afternoons. 'Look, there's a pepper-tree,' I'd say to him when I saw one.

'By golly, boy, that's only a little runt of a tree,' my dad would say. 'They don't grow so well in the city. Too much smoke, by golly. You ought to see them out west where I come from.'

My father was a tall, thin man with sad brown eyes and a head full of dreams. That was why he wanted to own a Rolls Royce one day. 'First our own house and then one day, if I'm lucky, I'll buy a Rolls Royce,' he would say.

Some of his friends thought this was a crazy dream.

'What would you do with a car like that, Peter?' they would say. 'Go and live with the millionaires?'

My father would stroke his long brown moustache, which had only a little white in it, and try to explain, but he could not make them understand. It has taken me all these years to realize what a Rolls Royce meant to him.

'It's not about what other people think of me,' he would say to my mother. 'No, by golly. I want to own a Rolls Royce because it is the most perfect piece of machinery made in the world. Why, a Rolls Royce—'

And then he would stop and feel for the right words to describe what he felt, and clumsily, lovingly, he would go on talking about how beautiful the engine was . . .

'What would a garage mechanic do with a Rolls Royce, I ask you!' my mother would say. 'I'd feel silly sitting up in it.'

At such times my mother would grab her brush and start cleaning the kitchen floor hard. My mother was a small round woman with brown hair which was pulled back from her face.

Like the pepper-tree, the Rolls Royce meant something

special to my father. He had been born in Tullama in the hot dry country where the mallee trees grow. His father was a builder and wanted his son to follow him. But my father's dream was to be an engineer. When he was eighteen, he had come to the city and begun to train with a mechanical engineer. He went to classes in the evening. But after two years he had to stop because of the damage to his eyes.

'It was all because of money,' he told me once. 'If you've got money, you can go to the university and learn things properly, become an engineer. I worked my eyes too hard, you see – I went to classes five nights a week and studied after I came home.'

After that, my father had to take any jobs that he could get, but always near machinery. 'I like playing about with machines, but I had no real training,' he said once.

He knew a lot, and most of it was things that you could only learn from books. He knew about rocks and how they were made. He could talk for hours about life on earth and how it began. He taught me more than all the teachers I ever had at school.

I remember him talking to my mother one night. I was twelve at the time, and he was forty-seven. Times were hard then, and my mother was worried about the future.

'Every day I hear of people losing their jobs,' she said.

'I haven't lost mine,' my father said, 'and if I do, I have a way of making some money.'

'I suppose it's another of your inventions, Peter? What is it this time?'

'That's my business,' he said. But he said it gently.

One thing that annoyed my mother was that my father was always losing money on his inventions. Another thing was that he was always filling the backyard with rubbish.

'What can you do with these silly little yards?' my father would say. 'Now, when I was a child at Tullama, we had a real backyard – why, it was enormous – it was as big—'

He'd stop there, unable to get the right word.

And so another piece of old machinery would arrive in the backyard. 'It was so cheap!' my father would say, delighted.

Soon after my father had said he had a plan to make some money, he went away early one Sunday morning. He came back at lunchtime in a Ford lorry. On the back of the Ford was a two-stroke engine. I came running out.

'I've bought it, Joe, by golly,' he told me.

And he had – both engine and lorry.

'So cheap! Forty pounds for them both – ten pounds now, and two pounds a month.'

My mother was cross when she heard.

'Why spend money on an engine when we need it to pay for the house, Peter?' she said.

'This'll pay for the house in no time, by golly,' my father said. 'And buy a lot of other things too.'

I knew by the way he looked up and over my mother's head that he was thinking of the Rolls Royce.

All that day he was very excited, walking round the engine, standing back and looking at it, then going up close. He spent all afternoon starting and stopping the engine. Every night when he came home from the garage during the

*'I've bought it, Joe, by golly,' Father told me. And he had
– both engine and lorry.*

next week, the first thing he did was look at the engine. He had some plan in his mind but he would not say what it was at first.

'Wait and see, Joe,' he said.

He didn't tell me his secret for over a week, although I knew he was thinking about nothing else. In the end, he came close to me in the kitchen one night, when my mother was in the bedroom, and whispered mysteriously, 'It's an invention for cleaning out wells, boy.'

'For cleaning out wells?'

He listened to hear if my mother was coming back.

'I'm putting a light out there tonight, boy,' he whispered. 'Come out later and I'll show you.'

My father's idea, he explained later, was a way of cleaning wells in country towns. You pushed a hard brush on the end of a pipe down the sides and along the bottom of the well. The pipe sucked up the dirt and you didn't lose much water from the well.

'Every country town has half a dozen wells, boy,' he said. 'The banks have them, and one or two of the richer families. Just like it was in Tullama. There's money in it because you can clean the well out without losing too much water. It's like finding gold – you can't lose.'

It sounded good to me.

'When do you start?' I asked.

'Soon, by golly,' he said. 'The job at the garage won't last much longer.'

He was right about that, but until the day she died my mother always had an idea that perhaps he had helped his job to come to an end. It was early in 1930 when my father left in the lorry, travelling west.

'You've got to go to places that don't get much rain,' he said.

'Like Tullama?' I said.

'Yes, like Tullama, by golly.'

I started thinking of the pepper-tree.

'Will you go to Tullama and see the pepper-tree?'

My father stroked his long moustache. Into his eyes came that look – the same look he had when he was thinking or talking about the Rolls Royce. He didn't answer for a bit.

'By golly, yes, boy, if I go there.'

Soon after this he started off. Every week brought a letter from him. He did well too. He was going west from Sydney and I followed the towns he spoke of on the map. One well took nearly a day, so in the larger towns he would stay over a week, in the smaller ones a day or a day and a half.

After he had been away for two months he was still a few towns away from Tullama, but you could see that he was going towards it.

'Him and that silly pepper-tree!' said my mother, but she didn't say it angrily. My father was sending her as much money as he used to bring home when he worked at the garage.

But as my father got closer to Tullama, my mother got a bit excited too. She made a little flag for me to put on the map. About this time a change came in my father's letters home. At first they had been happy and excited, but now they were quieter. He didn't talk so much about the money he was making, or say anything about the Rolls. Perhaps excitement was making him quieter as he got nearer to the pepper-tree, I thought.

'I know what it is,' my mother said. 'He's not getting proper meals. He's too old to be off on his own like this. He's not taking care of himself, I'm sure. And without a real bed to sleep in – only the back of that lorry.'

I thought the day would never come, but soon my dad had only one town to do before he would reach Tullama. His letters usually arrived on a Tuesday – he wrote home on Sundays – but around this time I waited for the post every day and was late for school three times. When a letter did come, I grabbed it from the postman's hand and hurried inside with it. It was from Tullama.

'All right, all right, slow down now, Joe,' my mother said. 'You and your pepper-tree!'

I read the letter over her elbow. There was only one page. There was nothing about the pepper-tree. Dad was well and making money, but he was thinking of returning soon.

I couldn't understand it.

On the next Tuesday there was no letter. Nor on the Wednesday. On the Thursday my father came home. He gave us a surprise, walking in at breakfast time. He said that he had sold the lorry and engine and come home by train. He looked tired and ashamed and somehow a lot older. I saw a lot more white in his moustache.

'The engine was no good,' he said. 'It kept breaking down. It cost me nearly everything I earned. I had to sell it to pay back the money I borrowed and buy a ticket home.'

'The engine was no good,' Father said. 'It kept breaking down.
It cost me nearly everything I earned.'

'Oh Peter,' my mother said, putting her arms round him. 'My poor love. I knew something was wrong.'

'Mother thought it was the food,' I said. 'She thought you weren't getting proper meals.'

'I'll make you a cup of tea, Peter,' my mother said. 'Then I'll get you some breakfast,'

'By golly, that sounds good,' my father said. This was the first time since he had walked in that he really sounded like my dad.

My mother hurried about the kitchen and my father talked a bit more. 'I thought I was going to do well at first,' he said. 'But the engine was too old. I was always fixing it – new this, new that. It ate up all the money I earned.'

He went on talking about the trip. Now that I was used to the idea that he was back, I wanted to know all about the pepper-tree.

'Did you see the pepper-tree, dad?'

'Yes, I saw it all right.'

I stood right in front of him as he sat at the table, but he was not looking at me but at something far away. He didn't answer for what seemed a long time.

'It was a little runt of a tree, boy – and a little backyard.'

He wouldn't say any more than that and he never spoke of the pepper-tree – or the Rolls – again.

The Empty Lunch-Tin

DAVID MALOUF

Retold by Christine Lindop

Some people see things that aren't real. Or maybe they are real; it's just that other people don't, or can't, see them. Who is right? Who do we believe? For some questions, perhaps there are just no answers.

The woman in this story is a mother whose child has died, but the remembered dead can live on in the mind and heart. And a memory can seem as real as a living person . . .

He had been there for a long time. He stood on the grass between the rose bush and the flowering tree, his shoulders down, his hands by his side. He stood very still with his face lifted towards the house, like someone who has rung the doorbell, got no answer, and hopes that somebody will appear at last at an upper window. He did not seem to notice the black currawongs that flew past him with sharp cries, or jumped about on the grass.

At first the shadow of the house had been at his feet, but it had moved back as the morning went on, and he stood now in a wide sunny space making his own shadow.

Behind him cars rushed along the road, taking children to school, and lorries delivered things to houses – there were no walls here; the garden was open to the street. He stood. And the only thing between him and the flowering tree was a water tap on a metal pipe that came up out of the grass.

At first, when she passed the glass wall of the dining-room and saw the thin figure with its short shadow on the grass, she had given a sharp little cry. Greg! It could so easily be him – he was just the right age. Doubting her own eyes, she had gone right up to the glass and stared. But Greg had been dead for seven years. Part of her knew this, the part that watched this stranger; but to the other part of her, Greg was still going on, a boy still growing into the fullness of his life, so that she knew just how he had looked at fifteen, seventeen, and now at twenty.

This young man was unlike Greg. He stood with his shoulders bent forward, and his clothes did not quite fit; he was shabby, not in a fashionable way, but because he was poor. In his loose trousers and wide hat, he looked like someone from the country or from another time. It was the way young men looked in her childhood, she thought, men who were out of work.

Thin and pale, with no coat, surely he had seen her come up to the glass and watch him, but he was not at all worried.

Yes, that was what he reminded her of: the Depression years, and those men, some with only one arm or one leg, who had waited on street corners in her childhood, wearing bits of uniform along with their old clothes, offering pencils or matches for sale. Sometimes, when you answered the back doorbell, you found one of them standing there on the step. What he wanted was a job: cutting the grass, clearing leaves from the roof, mending shoes . . . When there was no job, they simply stood, as this man stood, waiting for the offer of a cup of tea with a slice of bread, or a few pennies – it didn't matter what or how much. What you offered was not so important; they wanted you to recognize them, to see that you and they were alike. As a child, in her country town, she had watched how her mother behaved towards those men, and she had thought to herself: *This is one of the things people do. There is a way of doing this so that a man can remain proud, and you can too.* But when she grew up, the Depression was over. Instead, there was the Second World War. She never had to use those things she had half learned.

She walked out now into the garden and looked at the young man, with just air, not glass, between them.

He still wasn't anyone she recognized, but he had moved a little, and as she stood there silently watching him for some time, she saw that he continued to move. He was turning with the sun, as a plant does. If he decided to stay, she thought, perhaps she would get used to him. After all, why a flowering tree and not a perfectly normal young man?

She went back into the house and decided to go on with her housework. The house didn't need it with only two of them in it, but each day she did it just the same. She began in the living room, cleaning and making things tidy, taking care not to touch the electronic chess machine that her husband loved so much. On a table of its own, with its own light next to it, it was a piece of machinery that she thought of as a difficult visitor that had come to stay. It spoke the moves for the chess pieces in a dry dead voice, like a man speaking from a grave, and once, in the days when she had disliked it, she had accidentally started it. She had already turned

*She walked out now into the garden and looked at the young man,
with just air, not glass, between them.*

away when the flat dull voice spoke to her. For a moment it seemed that some lifeless thing in the room had suddenly decided to make contact with her. Well, it didn't shock her so much now, but she still avoided it.

She finished the living room, and without going to the window again went straight to the bathroom. She cleaned round the bath, the shower, and the toilet, then walked straight through to the living room and looked.

He was still there and had turned a quarter of a circle. She saw his thin figure from the side. But what was happening? He had no shadow. The metal tap made a shadow on the grass, and the young man didn't. It took a minute, a frightening minute, for her to see that the dark line on the grass was not the shadow of the tap, but a place where water had fallen. So that was all right. It was midday.

She did a strange thing then. She went straight into the kitchen, found butter, flour and sugar, and made some biscuits with whole peanuts in them, working fast and enjoying the old habits of cooking.

They were biscuits that had no special name. She had learned to make them when she was just a child, from a girl who had worked for them in the country. As she mixed the biscuits and spooned them onto paper to go in the cooker, she felt that she was becoming her younger self, someone who moved more lightly, more surely. She hadn't made these biscuits – hadn't felt able to make them – since Greg died. Now, while they were cooking and filling the house with their sweet, warm smell, she did another thing that she had not planned to do. She went to Greg's bedroom at the end of the hall and began to take down from the wall the flags he had won for swimming, the green one with gold letters, the purple one, the blue, and put them carefully on the bed. She brought a box from under the stairs and packed them in the bottom. Then she cleared the bookshelf and took down his little planes, and put them in the box as well. From his desk she took pencils, a box of cards, magazines, notebooks, all his boyish things, put them in the box and carried it out. Then she took clean sheets and made the bed.

By now the biscuits were ready to come out of the cooker. She counted them. There were twenty-three. Without looking outside, she opened the kitchen window and left the biscuits in front of the open window to cool. Then she went back and sat on Greg's bed.

She looked round the empty walls. What would a young man of twenty put on them, she wondered. It was painful to discover that she could not guess.

Then another figure came into her head out of the past.

In her middle years at school there had been a boy who sat two desks in front of her called Stevie Caine. She had always felt sorry for him because he lived alone with an aunt and was poor. The father had worked for the railway but lost his job after an accident and killed himself. It was Stevie Caine that this young man reminded her of. His shoulders too had been narrow and bent forward, his face unusually pale, his wrists bony. Stevie's hair was pale and dull and he smelled of washing soap. Too poor to go to the cinema on Saturday afternoons, or to have a radio, he could not join in the excited talk of the other children. When they ate their lunch he sat by himself on the far side of the yard, and she alone had guessed the reason: it was because the metal lunch-tin that his father had carried to the railway had nothing in it, or at best a slice of bread. But poor as he was, Stevie had not been bitter – that was the thing that had most surprised her. And his face sometimes, when he was excited, shone with such pleasure and sweetness that she wanted to reach out and touch his skin gently to feel the warmth. But perhaps he would misunderstand her gentle feelings for him – he would think she was in love with him, or, worse, felt sorry for him. So she did nothing.

Stevie Caine had left school when he was just fourteen and went like his father to work at the railway. She had seen him sometimes in his railway worker's uniform. The black hat made his face look even bonier, and he carried the same old lunch-tin. But he refused to be bitter or miserable, and that kept alive her gentle feelings towards him. Even now, years later, she could see the back of his thin neck. If she had the chance now, she would reach out and touch the rough skin, no longer caring if she was misunderstood.

When he was eighteen he had immediately joined the army and was immediately killed; she had seen it in the papers – just the name.

And this young man looked like Stevie Caine – Stevie as she had last seen him, in his soft hat and his railway worker's uniform. She had never known him well, but she had never forgotten. There were two kinds of injustice, she thought. One kind is cruel and can be changed; the other kind is when a thirteen-year-old boy is knocked off his bicycle and dies, and that cannot be changed. She remembered Stevie Caine because of this, and because of his empty lunch-tin. It was too late now, but she wanted to fill it with biscuits with whole peanuts in them that had no special name.

She went out quickly now (the young man was still there on the grass beyond the window) and counted the biscuits, which were cool enough to put away. There were twenty-three, just as before.

He stayed there all afternoon and was still there in the shadows when Jack came in. She was almost certain now of what the young man was, but she didn't want it proved. How awful if you walked up to someone, put your hand out to see if it would go through him, and it didn't.

They had tea, and Jack, after a shy worried look towards her, which she pretended not to see, took one of the biscuits and slowly ate it. She watched. He was trying not to show how desperately sad he felt. Poor Jack!

Twenty-two.

Later, while he sat playing chess and the mechanical voice told him what moves he should make for it, she went to the window and looked out. It was, very gently, raining, and the streetlights were softened. Slow cars passed, making soft sounds on the wet road.

The young man stood there in the same place. His shabby clothes were now completely wet, and on the edge of his hat drops of water shone brightly in the light.

'Mustn't it be awful,' she said, 'to be out there on a night like this, and have nowhere to go? There must be so many of them, just standing about in the rain, or sleeping in it.'

There were two of them, alike but different; both pale and hopeless,
with thin shoulders, wearing shabby clothes.

Something in her voice, some feeling that deeply touched and worried him, made the man leave his game and come to her side. They stood together for a moment in front of the dark wall of glass. Then she turned, looked into his face and did something strange. She reached out towards him and her hand bumped against his chest – that is how he thought of it: a bump. It was the strangest thing! A sudden fear seemed to leave her, and she kissed him.

I have so much, is what she thought to herself.

Next morning, alone again, she cleared away the breakfast and made a shopping list. Then she went to the window.

It was a fine clear day, and there were two of them, alike but different; both pale and hopeless, with thin shoulders, wearing shabby clothes. They did not appear to be together. There was nothing to show that they were connected, or that the first one had called the second one up from somewhere. But there were two of them just the same, suggesting a plan of some kind. Tomorrow, she guessed, there would be four, and the next day sixteen – until there was not enough room for them on the grass. There must be millions of them to come; they would fill up the street, and the next street – with no room for cars any more – and then the city, until a large part of the earth was covered. This was just the start.

She didn't feel worried. The two figures simply stood there. But she thought she would not tell Jack until he noticed it. Then they would do together what was necessary.

Cross Currents

MARION HALLIGAN

Retold by Christine Lindop

Teachers work very hard. As well as all the usual teaching in the classroom, they often do extra things – helping with sports, running clubs, taking students on excursions.

Martha and Linda are teachers in Australia. They are on their way to Sydney, for an exciting week in that great city. Maybe a little too exciting, because travelling with them are twenty sixteen-year-old schoolgirls . . .

It was a line of schoolgirls. Unexpected in that time and place, but very recognizable. A long line of girls walking in pairs, more or less, making their way across the bridge into Victoria Street. Twenty schoolgirls, aged about sixteen, mostly pretty, dressed in fashionable hot-weather clothes. Martha, watching from across the street, noticed in surprise how alike they all looked, even in their different clothes.

'You must be completely crazy, Martha. Taking twenty sixteen-year-olds to Kings Cross for a week! You'll have to watch them every minute. It's a sex supermarket down there, you know.'

'That's why it's quite safe. People who go to Kings Cross go there for business – they expect to pay. They aren't interested in a bunch of giggling schoolgirls. The innocent are safe.'

'And how innocent are twenty schoolgirls? On their own, maybe, but when they're together in a group?'

'They're from good families, you know. Private school, rich parents – they've had it all. If that makes any difference.'

'What are you going to do?'

'The usual. Sightseeing – the Opera House, the Rocks, Vaucluse House. A little shopping for fun. But mostly culture, history, education. And a play: *Measure for Measure* at the Seymour Centre.'

'Wow. What will they get from that?'

'Quite a lot. Shakespeare is wonderful theatre, you know. It has a great effect even on those who don't really understand it.'

'They'll wear school uniform, of course.'

'No chance! None of them would come. A week in their own clothes – that's why they want to come on this excursion.'

The trip hot and dusty, the hotel a welcome end to the journey. A problem with the rooms: the girl on the desk, unpretty and unhelpful ('She must be sleeping with the manager,' said Linda), unable to find an answer. The girls, tired but excited, waiting in the hotel foyer. Martha, Linda, and the bus-driver patiently explaining, again and again, the manager solving the problem imperfectly, and the girls sent, five in each group, to their rooms. Then a dull dinner in the large dining-room.

And afterwards, a little walk in the cool of the evening to see the wonders of Kings Cross – innocent country girls meeting the city, hot and alive with sin. Along Darlinghurst Road, down Macleay Street, the girls staring and talking. *Don't go down that street Mrs Ambrose it doesn't look safe, hurry up Mrs Baudin don't get behind you never know what'll happen.* The girls no problem, staying together, afraid of getting lost. Open-eyed at the buying and selling of girls, some in short skirts, others in party dresses, and at the men who walked in groups, talking, laughing, looking at the girls for sale. Annoyed when the men recognized them for what they were, calling *School's out!* and *Learnt to read yet?* when they hoped they looked like women of the world. Their clothes were no different from those worn by many of the prostitutes, and as a group they were bright and confident, but anyone could see that they were not for sale. Martha and Linda were as fascinated by the business as their girls; Linda was sure it was more in the open now than on her last visit two years ago.

Later, she walked back to a café with two of the girls who wanted to buy chocolate – *That awful dinner, we're terribly hungry* – realizing too late that it was cigarettes they wanted. A tall girl came towards them, walking quickly, fastening a wide silver belt around her black dress. Pausing beside them, saying, *Do you want a girl, sweetheart?* to the man standing behind them. What was the answer? Linda was too polite to turn and look, though she really wanted to. Allow them their privacy; don't stare. Move the girls along. Stay in control. A cultural excursion, of great social interest.

Back at the hotel, three girls standing on the front steps, waiting for aunts to take them out, dressed for the heat in the shortest, lightest clothes.

'I think you should wait inside, girls. You know what standing in doorways means here.'

Immediately they are gone, into the once grand foyer.

How grateful the two teachers were for the wine that Martha, who had been on such excursions before, had packed in her suitcase. The girls safely in their rooms, the exhausted teachers and bus-driver drank cold white wine and beer, discussing the ways of schoolgirls. The bus-driver, who had done many such trips, knew what his job was: he was the father, the man, the strong one if needed. He also knew that half the girls had their eyes on him, the only man around them all week. And he was good-looking, nice body, strong muscles.

He thought the teachers did a wonderful job and needed plenty of laughs. He told them endless stories in his own rough and lively language. Linda and Martha, English teachers, were fascinated by the awfulness of his grammar and the liveliness of his words; they hadn't met anyone quite like him before.

One of his stories was about having his picture in a women's magazine. They wanted to take a photo of him at the wheel of his bus with no clothes on. Of course they would arrange the photo to show his handsome body, but the steering wheel would . . . you know, cover up, hide . . . anything you shouldn't see. He refused the offer, which was lucky, because in fact it wasn't true – it was just a clever joke arranged by some of his friends, who had laughed about it for months afterwards.

The only problem with the bus-driver's stories was the difficulty of making him stop. Linda once went and had a shower and got into bed and still he went on talking about his wife and children and life on the road, as the night got shorter and they hoped desperately for sleep.

Samantha, Amanda, Felicity, three Jennies, Belinda, Annabel, two Fionas, Sybil, Catherine, Clair . . . twenty girls still. The Rocks with its narrow old streets full of history far too hot, and the girls getting tired on the guided tour. Shopping in town . . . *don't forget to look at the Strand Arcade, girls, and be back here in one hour exactly, the bus can't wait in Pitt Street* . . . Elizabeth Bay House, a grand historical building, and then . . . *can't we stay inside here all day, it's so cool, can't we go for a swim, it's too hot, sightseeing's boring* . . . The bus-driver taking them swimming . . . *Ugh, it's salt water* . . . but half of them choosing to lie about in their hotel rooms with clothes and drink cans lying everywhere, the air thick with cigarette smoke. Too difficult to stop the girls smoking – so they smoked, but not in front of the teachers. Trying on the hats they'd bought and the bracelets and tops and shoes; the shopping the bribe, the part they'd liked best. Vaucluse House, another grand old house, was terrific, said some, but most, living in a closed little world of the present moment and their own bodies, had taken very little notice of it.

The narrow old streets full of history far too hot, and the girls getting tired on the guided tour.

The play: *Measure for Measure*. Shakespeare, as you know, girls. This is the story of the play – read it so you'll know what's happening. Notice the ideas behind the play. How to live a good life. What's right, and what's wrong. Doing the right thing in front of other people and the wrong thing in your private life – and the other way round. Sex controlling everybody and everything. Guilt. And of course hypocrisy – saying one thing and doing another. What's the difference between a pimp, who lives off the money his prostitutes earn, and a good man who falls into sin, but pretends he is still a good man?

'What's Shakespeare like?' said the bus-driver.

'Fantastic,' said Martha. 'It doesn't matter if you don't understand every word, it's such exciting theatre you get involved in it.'

'Perhaps I should try it, for once. You think I'd like it?'

'You might . . .'

'Well, I'll try it, why not?'

Unfortunately, this was Shakespeare with a difference. A group of serious actors had worked alone on the play for six months and the result was just actors and words. They wore everyday modern clothes, and just had a couple of chairs and a table. Men played some women's parts, and women played some men's parts, and the words were spoken without excitement or feeling.

At half past eight Martha looked at her watch and thought

what an awfully long time it was until ten past eleven. This way of doing Shakespeare was not a success. There was no life, no movement, even the language sounded dull and flat. Martha felt terrible guilt for bringing the schoolgirls to see it – guilt for giving them a boring evening, and for proving to them that, yes, Shakespeare was dull and meant nothing these days.

After the first half of the play she and Linda apologized to all the girls they could see, and the bus-driver.

'Shakespeare's not usually like this,' they said. 'We didn't know it was going to be so flat, so colourless.'

'Oh, it's all right,' the girls said. 'We quite like it.'

'Can you understand it?' Linda asked.

'Oh yes. Well, not every word. But you can tell what's happening.'

'Mm. It's quite exciting. I can't wait to see what happens.'

'That Angelo's really nasty. He's good though.'

'I like Pompey, he's so funny.'

'And Lucio – he's great.'

'What about Claudio?'

'Isabella's a bit weak. Quite annoying really. Specially when Claudio's so brave. But they're all really good actors.'

'Mm. I've seen that Mariana woman on TV.'

'In Shakespeare's time the actors wore fantastic clothes,' said Martha. 'And the acting was full of life and fun.'

'Oh. Well, this is pretty good.'

How extraordinary, to be right after all. Linda, who had seen *Measure for Measure* lots of times before, thought that it was impossible to kill Shakespeare. The words were there, a bit flat, but spoken with intelligence. Even the bus-driver was enjoying it. Feeling less guilty, Martha and Linda quite enjoyed the second half of the play.

It was their last night. After the play the bus-driver took them for a drive to see the city lights. The girls were restless when they got back to their rooms, giggling and making supper and refusing to calm down. The teachers made final checks.

'Hurry up and get to sleep, girls, it's a big day tomorrow.'

'We'll sleep in the bus, Mrs Ambrose. It's our last night, we can't sleep through it.'

Martha and Linda were so tired after the week that sleep seemed like a lost habit. They drank the last of the white wine and ate cheese and olives for supper. They talked, about the week, about the girls, about teaching, all the things there normally wasn't time for. It was late when they actually stopped. Martha was in bed, enjoying a short read before sleep, Linda was in the bathroom in the dark with the window wide open, enjoying the wonderful tourist's view of Sydney, the silver sails of the Opera House, the strong shape of the bridge against the pale city sky.

There was a lot of noise outside. At the back of the hotel there was a piece of unused ground; tonight it had cars on it, and groups of people came and went, talking, laughing, shrieking, pretending to drive into each other; cars stopped and started, doors banged. Nobody was serious. There was a lot of giggling, too, nearby. Linda put her head out, carefully; the window was low and it was the fourth floor. Parked below was a car, long and low, fast and shiny; two men in it were looking up, and talking, talking to three heads looking out of the second floor, a little to Linda's right.

'What are you smoking?' asked one of the men.

'Benson and Hedges,' said one of the girls.

'Oh, is that all?'

'Why, have you got anything better?'

'Come down and we'll show you.'

'Show us what?'

'Come for a drive. We'll have a good time.'

Linda hurried back into the bedroom to the sleepy Martha.

'Those horrible girls. Halfway out of the window, talking to men. Pimps, probably.'

Martha went into the bathroom, looked out, listened.

'Hell. What a group of tarts,' she said.

'I suppose they think they're safe, and out of reach,' said Linda.

'Ooh, I'd like to do something,' Martha said. 'Drop something on them. Frighten them a bit.'

'Good idea. Something not too damaging and hard, but not too light either.'

They looked about. Books, papers, wine box – not suitable. The conversation went on below, the girls not going down, but letting the men think they might.

'I know. Soap.'

The perfect thing. A small piece of hotel soap. Heavy enough to fall, without doing too much damage. Linda looked out, dropped it. There was a loud dull noise as soap hit metal, and an angry shout.

'Hey, what the hell do you think you're doing? Bloody women . . .'

'We didn't do that!' (The girls, innocent, annoyed.)

'The hell you didn't.'

The car left in a storm of angry engine noise. Martha and Linda bent over with silent laughter in the dark bathroom, feeling like silly schoolgirls themselves.

Meanwhile, some girls on the fifth floor, above and to the left, began to giggle. The heads on the second floor turned upwards and shrieked with anger.

'You dropped that! You stupid bloody—'

'We didn't.'

'You did.'

The voices got angry. Each group believed the other was lying, as neither group realized that the soap had come from somebody else. The shouting got louder and louder. Martha wondered if they should put a stop to the noise; it was after two o'clock. But if she called out of the window, the girls would realize what had happened, and it was a very long way, up and down stairs, to walk to the girls' rooms.

'We'll give them five minutes, then go and quieten them down.'

Five minutes was enough. The girls stopped shouting rude things at each other, and the teachers went to bed.

Their room was next to the bathroom and above the car park too. It was hard to sleep with the noise of people still enjoying themselves. Martha lay half asleep, unable to

Some girls on the fifth floor began to giggle. The heads on the second floor turned upwards and shrieked with anger.

shut out the noise, and was quickly awake when another conversation started.

The second floor again. And three men, not very young, in the middle of the road.

'No good up there. You'll have to come down.'

'Why should we?'

'You'll have to come and see. Or would you like us to come up?'

'Yeah. We'll come up. What room?'

'I'm having the one in the middle.'

'The one on the end for me. You remember, when I come up.'

'Which room, eh, girls?'

The girls giggled, whispered together, called down answers. It's the oldest conversation in the world, thought Martha, a man talking to a woman. But do the girls realize that the men are expecting to pay? With sudden alarm she thought of the fire-escape stairs, with their doors next to the girls' rooms. The doors were locked to the outside, but could be opened from inside – you could get out that way, but not in. But suppose that somebody had forgotten to lock them. Or somebody opened them. The girls were silly enough for anything tonight.

She put her head out the window. She spoke in a clear ringing icy schoolteacher's voice.

'Would you *children* pull your heads in and go to bed!'

The girls disappeared at once. Surprise from the men, then laughter, as they went on their way.

The girls were tired next morning, silently sorry about the night before. The two teachers took them to the zoo, and swimming at Manly, before the long drive home. Martha and Linda went into a pub to use the toilet and found the floor covered in blood; a girl had tried to kill herself in there, they were told. The girls gave the teachers great armfuls of flowers as thanks; the driver put them in the bus refrigerator. The flowers didn't last long in the hot weather, but it was a kind thought. They'd had a lovely time, the girls said, they'd really enjoyed themselves, and learnt a lot about culture, history, and human beings. Everybody agreed that the excursion had been a great success.

GLOSSARY

ancestor a person in your family who lived a long time ago

backyard the area behind a house, including the garden

barefoot not wearing anything on your feet

bastard *(taboo, offensive)* a rude word for someone, especially a man; *(slang)* a word sometimes used in an affectionate way

biscuit a small flat dry cake

bloody *(slang, offensive)* a word used to emphasize a comment or an angry statement

bump *(v)* to hit a part of your body against something

camp *(in this story)* an area where Aboriginal people live, often with poor housing and conditions

chess a game in which two people move pieces on a board with black and white squares following special rules

culture the ideas and beliefs of a particular society or country

Depression the period in the 1930s when many people were without jobs

duck a bird that lives near water with short legs and a wide beak

electronic *(of a machine)* having many small parts that control the electricity that makes the machine work

excursion a journey made by a group of people for pleasure

fascinate to interest somebody very much

fist a hand when it is tightly closed, with the fingers bent in

flour a fine white powder made from wheat

foyer a large open space inside the entrance of a hotel

giggle to laugh in a silly way

golly (by golly) *(old-fashioned)* used to express surprise

grab to take something suddenly or roughly with your hand

heaven the place where some people believe God is

hell (what the hell?) used to express anger or surprise

homestead a house with the land and buildings around it

humpy *(Australian English)* a roughly built Aboriginal house

hut a small, simply built house or shelter

injustice the fact that a situation is unfair, unjust

kettle a container in which water is boiled

key one of the wooden parts that you press to play a piano

landscape everything you can see across a large area of land

lean *(v)* to rest against something for support

magpie a black and white bird with a noisy cry

mate a friendly word for a man, used by men to each other

Missus *(old-fashioned)* Mrs; used by servants to a female employer

nigger *(taboo)* a very offensive word for a black person

note a single sound made by a musical instrument

original existing from the beginning of a particular time

peacock a large male bird with a long blue and green tail

peanut a small kind of nut that grows underground

pioneer one of the first people to go and live in a particular area

prostitute a person who has sex for money

pyjamas a loose jacket and trousers worn in bed

Rolls Royce a large, very expensive, famous British car

rooster an adult male chicken

runt the smallest and weakest of a family of young animals

Rusilla a rosella, a kind of Australian parakeet

sergeant a police officer

sex the act of making love

shabby in poor condition after being used a lot

shriek *(v)* to give a loud high shout

sin an offence against a religious or moral law

slab a thick flat piece of wood

snake a reptile with a very long thin body and no legs

spirit a ghost; or an imaginary creature that lives in trees, etc.

store   a shop; or a place where things of a particular kind are
   kept
stroke *(v)* to move your hand gently over something; *(n)* a single
   movement
stubbies *(Australian English)*   small fat bottles of beer
suck   to take liquid out of something
tart *(slang)*   a prostitute
tribe   a group of people of the same race, with the same
   customs, language, etc., living in a particular area
trigger   the part of a gun that you press in order to fire it
triumph   a feeling of great satisfaction that you get from success
verandah   a platform with an open front and a roof, built on the
   side of a house on the ground floor
wagon   a vehicle with four wheels, pulled by horses
well *(n)*   a deep hole in the ground from which you get water
wipe   to remove liquid or dirt from something using a cloth

ABORIGINAL WORDS
used in the story *Going Home*

boya   money
Nyoongah   a word used by Aboriginal people in the south-west
   of Western Australia to speak about themselves
unna   a word at the end of a question, meaning 'Isn't it?' or 'Isn't
   that right?'
wadgula   white people
woodarchi   evil spirit

ACTIVITIES

Before Reading

Before you read the stories, read the introductions at the
beginning, then use these activities to help you think about the
stories. How much can you guess or predict?

1 *Because of the Rusilla* (story introduction page 1). Try to guess
what good and bad experiences the children have.

   1 a) They find some money.   b) Somebody gives them
      presents.   c) They make a new friend.
   2 a) They get into a fight.   b) They are not allowed into a
      shop.   c) Some white children are horrible to them.

2 *The Weeping Fig* (story introduction page 14). Choose ideas
(one or more) to explain the importance of the weeping fig.

   1 A young farming family survives by eating its fruit and
     escaping from the sun under its branches.
   2 The family uses its wood to build their first house.
   3 It reminds someone of the difficult times that his family
     survived in the past.

3 *Going Home* (story introduction page 23). What will Billy find
at the camp? Choose the words you think will be best.

   1 The houses are *modern / rough / clean.*
   2 His mother *cries / smiles / turns away* when she sees him.
   3 White people are *rude to / kind to /not interested in* him.

4 *The Pepper-Tree* (story introduction page 38). What do you think will happen in this story? Choose the best words.

  1 *Joe* / *His father* will look for the pepper-tree.

  2 He *will* / *will not* find it.

  3 This will make him feel *pleased* / *disappointed* / *angry*.

5 *The Empty Lunch-Tin* (story introduction page 48). Talk about your answers to these questions.

  1 A lunch-tin is a box of food . . .

    a) taken away from a restaurant.

    b) which you take to work or school.

    c) for an outdoor meal.

  2 The story is about . . .

    a) a ghost.   b) a dead person.   c) a dream.

6 *Cross Currents* (story introduction page 58). What do you think? Discuss your ideas.

Would you like to be a teacher taking sixteen-year-old schoolgirls on a trip to a city? Why, or why not?

7 What do you know about Australia? Choose the best words.

Aboriginal people came to Australia *400,000* / *40,000* years ago, and the first British settlers arrived in the *seventeenth* / *eighteenth* century. Two thirds of the country is *forest* / *desert*, and most of Australia's *20* / *40* million people live near the *sea* / *mountains* in the *south and east* / *north and west*. In recent years people have come from *African* / *Asian* countries to live here.

ACTIVITIES

After Reading

1 Here are the thoughts of six characters (one from each story). Who is thinking, in which story, and what has just happened in the story?

1 'We've got the drink – but what can I get him for a present? I gotta get him a present! He's twenty-one, unna? Gotta be something special. But where am I going to find that round here? Oh, wait a minute . . .'

2 'Well, that wasn't what I would call a conversation! The man was almost rude. All he was interested in was his dull old buildings. Anyway, if he wants to walk around in this heat staring at old huts, that's just fine by me. But he'll be on his own.'

3 'I think they do a fantastic job, I really do. I wouldn't do it if you paid me! But it must be hard, being with kids all day. You need a bit of adult conversation after that. So that's what I try and do, and they love it. They can't get enough of my stories!'

4 'When that big boy threw our brother on the ground like that, I wanted to kill him. He's just a little boy, and he isn't very strong. I'm glad uncle came along when he did, but I am not going to cry. I am absolutely not, not, not, not, not going to cry . . .'

5 'When I came home and smelt that smell, my heart nearly broke. She hasn't made those biscuits for years. My poor love, does she think she'll bring him back somehow? That taste – it brings tears to my eyes. So many memories . . .'

6 'Something isn't right. It's not what he says, it's what he doesn't say. Why doesn't he mention it? He's been talking about it for years, and suddenly – nothing at all! I really don't know what to say to the boy. It's a mystery, all right.'

2 Complete this conversation between Ama and Lal from *Because of the Rusilla* about Lal's present from the white lady. Use as many words as you like.

AMA: So tell me about your visit to the lady's house, Lal.

LAL: When Uncle Seyed left, _____.

AMA: And what did you do there?

LAL: We all did different things. I _____.

AMA: So what happened when Uncle Seyed came back?

LAL: The lady _____ and we told her _____.

AMA: But I don't understand – why did she give you a kettle?

LAL: Because _____.

AMA: Like your Rusilla? What do you mean?

LAL: You put _____.

AMA: And why did she think the kettle was a good present for you?

LAL: Because _____.

AMA: Then she is a very kind lady. Let's go and listen to your new Rusilla. I must hear this!

3 Here are two passages about the stories in which trees are important – *The Weeping Fig* and *The Pepper-Tree*. Choose one suitable word to fill each gap. Then say which story each passage is about.

1 This tree grew in the man's _____ at his childhood home, but he _____ not seen it for years. He _____ about it a lot, saying it _____ bigger and greener than any city _____. It seemed to have a special ___ in his heart – perhaps this was _____ it brought back memories of happy _____ as a child. However, when he _____ back to see it in later _____, as an adult, he was very _____, because he discovered the tree was _____ enormous nor special.

2 This tree was more than a _____ years old, and part of the _____ of this man's family. His great-grandmother _____ planted it, and she was buried _____ it with two of her children. _____ he stood in the tree's cool ____, the man felt proud that the _____ had survived. It meant that his _____ had left their mark on the _____.

Passage 1 is about the tree in _____
Passage 2 is about the tree in _____

4 What do you think happens in *Going Home* after the story ends? Read the notes below, and choose which ending you prefer. Then write a short paragraph to make a new ending, using the notes.

1 Rennie confesses / Billy freed / goes home to city / never returns to camp / has white friends and girlfriend

2 Rennie says nothing / Billy goes to prison / angry because
   in prison but brother stole watch / leaves prison and lives in
   city / old life gone / drunk like Aunty Rose
3 Peters taken to police station / picks out Rennie, not Billy,
   from line / Rennie goes to prison / Billy returns to city /
   sends money for Rennie's child

5 **The ending of *The Empty Lunch-Tin* is very mysterious, and
   can be understood in different ways. Choose the one you like
   best from these ideas and say why you prefer it, or write your
   own explanation of the ending.**

   1 Jack will never notice anything, because the young men on
      the grass are only real in his wife's mind.
   2 The young men are the ghosts of all young men who were
      killed in wars.
   3 Because of her long sadness at her son's death, the woman
      now has a special sixth sense and can see things that other
      people can't.
   4 The woman now accepts her son's death, but will always
      be able to see the ghosts of people who have been killed.

6 **Imagine that you are one of the girls in *Cross Currents*. Write
   a postcard home about your trip. Use these notes to help you.**

   · Dear Mum / hot journey in bus / tired / bus-driver nice
   · Sydney great / visit to Rocks / old houses
   · shopping in town / excited / new clothes / shoes
   · visit to theatre tonight / Shakespeare / boring?
   · home soon / love

7 Which of the characters in these stories would you like to . . .

   1 give some advice to?

   2 invite to a party?

   3 take home to meet your parents?

   4 sit next to on a long flight?

   5 never meet at all?

8 Here is a short poem (a kind of poem called a haiku) about one of the stories. Which of the six stories is it about?

> *Death is all around*
> *but the proud tree still survives*
> *giving green coolness.*

Here is another haiku, about the same story.

> *The tree she cared for*
> *waves its thick green leaves above*
> *her last resting place.*

A haiku is a Japanese poem, which is always in three lines, and the three lines always have 5, 7, and 5 syllables each, like this:

| The | tree | she | cared | for | = 5 syllables

| waves | its| thick | green | leaves | a | bove | = 7 syllables

| her | last | rest | ing | place | = 5 syllables

Now write your own haiku, one for each of the other five stories. Think about what each story is really about. What are the important ideas for you? Remember to keep to three lines of 5, 7, 5 syllables each.

ABOUT THE AUTHORS

MENA ABDULLAH AND RAY MATHEW

Mena Abdullah (1930–), the daughter of a Punjabi immigrant to Australia, grew up on a sheep farm on the Gwydir river in New South Wales. She worked for many years at the Commonwealth Scientific and Research Organization, where she met Ray Mathew (1929–2002). Together they wrote a volume of short stories called *The Time of the Peacock* (1965), which includes *Because of the Rusilla*. Ray Mathew lived much of his life outside Australia as a playwright and art critic. Mena Abdullah has continued to write short stories; many are about growing up as a Muslim in Australia. Although she has a Punjabi background herself, she has said, 'I am Australian, and that is all there is to it.'

JUDITH WRIGHT

Judith Wright (1915–2000) is best known for her poetry, although she also wrote short stories and children's books. Many people consider her to be one of the best Australian poets of the twentieth century. She had a deep love of the Australian landscape, and worked for many years to protect the environment and to fight for the rights of the Aboriginal people. She has been called 'the conscience of Australia', and she said about herself, 'I've been a writer all of my life and a conservationist for far too much of it.'

ARCHIE WELLER

Archie Weller (1957–) grew up on a farm in the southwest of Australia. His first novel *Day of the Dog* was published in 1981 and was later made into the film *Blackfellas* in 1993. Both the book and the film won awards. A second novel, *Land of the Golden Clouds*, was published in 1998. He has also written poems, short stories, and plays. He thinks it is important for Aboriginals to write about their experience of life because 'people die and take their feelings with them but the written word stays on forever.'

DAL STIVENS

Dal Stivens (1911–1997) worked as a journalist, court reporter, and public servant before becoming a full-time writer in 1950. His best-known novel is *A Horse of Air,* and he also wrote short stories. He said, 'Short stories must grow naturally out of the age in which you live', and he based the main character in *The Pepper-Tree* on a man he met in his childhood who came to town to clean out wells. This man collected fossils, and patiently answered the curious boy's many questions. Stivens had a great love of painting, and natural history, and was the founder of the Australian Society of Authors.

DAVID MALOUF

David Malouf (1934–) was born in Queensland to a Lebanese father and an English mother. In the 1960s he spent some years in England, working as a teacher. He now lives in Sydney. He began his writing career by publishing poems, and has since written novels, short stories, and libretti for operas. He is best known for his novels and short stories, many of which have won literary prizes. *Remembering Babylon* (1993), a novel set in nineteenth-century Australia, won the first International IMPAC Dublin Literary Award in 1996. His short story collections include *Every Move You Make* (2007). When asked in a radio interview about the art of writing, he said, 'Resurrecting things in memory and making them present and alive again is in fact one of the things that is an essentially human activity, and that's what a lot of writing is about.'

MARION HALLIGAN

Marion Halligan (1940–) was born in Newcastle on the east coast of Australia but has lived in Canberra for many years. She is well known for novels such as *The Fog Garden* and *The Golden Dress*, and has won many awards for her writing. She has also written books of essays, non-fiction, and short stories, as well as a children's book, and has a long and distinguished history of writing about food. In an interview she said, 'Good short stories are actually very hard to write, and can be quite hard to read . . . Ideally, they're suited to people who want to spend a bit of time reading and a lot of time thinking . . .'

OXFORD BOOKWORMS LIBRARY

Classics • Crime & Mystery • Factfiles • Fantasy & Horror
Human Interest • Playscripts • Thriller & Adventure
True Stories • World Stories

The OXFORD BOOKWORMS LIBRARY provides enjoyable reading in English, with a wide range of classic and modern fiction, non-fiction, and plays. It includes original and adapted texts in seven carefully graded language stages, which take learners from beginner to advanced level. An overview is given on the next pages.

All Stage 1 titles are available as audio recordings, as well as over eighty other titles from Starter to Stage 6. All Starters and many titles at Stages 1 to 4 are specially recommended for younger learners. Every Bookworm is illustrated, and Starters and Factfiles have full-colour illustrations.

The OXFORD BOOKWORMS LIBRARY also offers extensive support. Each book contains an introduction to the story, notes about the author, a glossary, and activities. Additional resources include tests and worksheets, and answers for these and for the activities in the books. There is advice on running a class library, using audio recordings, and the many ways of using Oxford Bookworms in reading programmes. Resource materials are available on the website www.oup.com/elt/bookworms

The *Oxford Bookworms Collection* is a series for advanced learners. It consists of volumes of short stories by well-known authors, both classic and modern. Texts are not abridged or adapted in any way, but carefully selected to be accessible to the advanced student.

You can find details and a full list of titles in the *Oxford Bookworms Library Catalogue* and *Oxford English Language Teaching Catalogues*, and on the website www.oup.com/elt/bookworms

THE OXFORD BOOKWORMS LIBRARY
GRADING AND SAMPLE EXTRACTS

STARTER • 250 HEADWORDS

present simple – present continuous – imperative –
can/cannot, must – *going to* (future) – simple gerunds ...

Her phone is ringing – but where is it?

Sally gets out of bed and looks in her bag. No phone. She looks under the bed. No phone. Then she looks behind the door. There is her phone. Sally picks up her phone and answers it. *Sally's Phone*

STAGE 1 • 400 HEADWORDS

... past simple – coordination with *and, but, or* –
subordination with *before, after, when, because, so* ...

I knew him in Persia. He was a famous builder and I worked with him there. For a time I was his friend, but not for long. When he came to Paris, I came after him – I wanted to watch him. He was a very clever, very dangerous man. *The Phantom of the Opera*

STAGE 2 • 700 HEADWORDS

... present perfect – *will* (future) – *(don't) have to, must not, could* –
comparison of adjectives – simple *if* clauses – past continuous –
tag questions – *ask/tell* + infinitive ...

While I was writing these words in my diary, I decided what to do. I must try to escape. I shall try to get down the wall outside. The window is high above the ground, but I have to try. I shall take some of the gold with me – if I escape, perhaps it will be helpful later. *Dracula*

STAGE 3 • 1000 HEADWORDS

... should, may present perfect continuous – *used to* – past perfect
– causative – relative clauses – indirect statements ...

Of course, it was most important that no one should see
Colin, Mary, or Dickon entering the secret garden. So Colin
gave orders to the gardeners that they must all keep away
from that part of the garden in future. *The Secret Garden*

STAGE 4 • 1400 HEADWORDS

*... past perfect continuous – passive (simple forms) –
would* conditional clauses – indirect questions –
relatives with *where/when* – gerunds after prepositions/phrases ...

I was glad. Now Hyde could not show his face to the world
again. If he did, every honest man in London would be proud
to report him to the police. *Dr Jekyll and Mr Hyde*

STAGE 5 • 1800 HEADWORDS

... future continuous – future perfect –
passive (modals, continuous forms) –
would have conditional clauses – modals + perfect infinitive ...

If he had spoken Estella's name, I would have hit him. I was so
angry with him, and so depressed about my future, that I could
not eat the breakfast. Instead I went straight to the old house.
Great Expectations

STAGE 6 • 2500 HEADWORDS

... passive (infinitives, gerunds) – advanced modal meanings –
clauses of concession, condition

When I stepped up to the piano, I was confident. It was as if I
knew that the prodigy side of me really did exist. And when I
started to play, I was so caught up in how lovely I looked that
I didn't worry how I would sound. *The Joy Luck Club*

MORE WORLD STORIES FROM BOOKWORMS